P. De Tracy

The Life of Saint Gaëtan

Founder of the Order of Théatins

P. De Tracy

The Life of Saint Gaëtan
Founder of the Order of Théatins

ISBN/EAN: 9783743408340

Manufactured in Europe, USA, Canada, Australia, Japa

Cover: Foto ©Raphael Reischuk / pixelio.de

Manufactured and distributed by brebook publishing software
(www.brebook.com)

P. De Tracy

The Life of Saint Gaëtan

THE

LIFE OF SAINT GAËTAN,

FOUNDER OF THE ORDER OF THÉATINS.

FROM A BIOGRAPHY OF THE SAINT BY

THE REVEREND P. DE TRACY,

PUBLISHED IN 1774, AND FROM

THE BOLLANDIST LIVES OF THE SAINTS.

"I exhort you afresh to propose to yourself continually the example of the Saints in all your actions, words, and thoughts. They are our Masters: we must learn in their school. They are our Brothers: we must resemble them. They are our Fathers: we must imitate them. Let their lives be models for ours. Let not their admirable lessons be one day a subject of confusion to us, nor expose us to a late repentance for having disdained to follow such sure and lofty guidance."—*Extract of Letter from St. Bernard to his Sister.*

TRANSLATED BY LADY HERBERT.

DUBLIN:

CHRISTOPHER SMYTH, 57, DAME-STREET.

MDCCCLXXIII.

PREFACE.

The name of Lady Herbert, so well known to Catholic readers, is in itself sufficient recommendation to this new publication which she presents to them in an English form.

Like St. Ignatius of Loyola, St. Philip Neri, and St. Charles Borromeo, St. Cajetan was raised up by God to oppose the evils brought on Christendom by the heresy of Luther. Born in 1480—three years before the apostate monk—St. Cajetan, by his holiness of life and apostolic preaching, prevented the spread of heresy and healed the corruption of morals. The only end our saint had in view was the greater glory of God, his zeal to promote which is shown in the adornment of the house of God and the exact observance of the ceremonial of the Church, by which means he raised the minds of the people to a due respect for God's majesty, excited by the splendour of His worship.

By promoting the frequentation of the Sacraments, and especially of the Holy Eucharist, so much attacked by heresy, he laid the foundation of solid and true devotion, and promoted the worship due to that holiest of sacraments.

The devotion of our saint to the Blessed Virgin was most filial. His confidence in God's providence was most striking, as shewn in his life, and the rules he laid down for his congregation. To carry out more fully these pious ends, and spread the devotion so dear to him, our Saint founded the Congregation of Clerics Regular—called after him, Théatins.

By founding seminaries where the young aspirants to the ecclesiastical state were imbued with the spirit and zeal of their holy founder, the sons of St. Cajetan spread widely the good begun by the saint, and continue to do so down to our own time.

The good done by St. Cajetan was nurtured by prayer, and owes its success to the fervent devotion of the saint. Ours is an age in which even good people are led away by what catches the eye, attach all importance to external work, and undervalue or make no account of a life hidden with God in prayer, when holy souls, away from the distractions of a busy world, devote their lives not only to their own sanctification but also to that of others. When the world forgets God, they are mindful of Him : when sinners provoke God's anger, they ask for pardon. When God's ministers are engaged in the external labours of the ministry, they, by their prayers prepare the way for them by obtaining the grace of conversion and perseverance for sinners.

St Teresa in her cloister had chiefly in view the salvation of souls. In the third chapter of the *Way of Perfection* she explains to her children how they, shut up in their convent, may labour for the salvation of souls, namely, by praying, suffering, performing acts of mortification, with the intention that the Lord may give to his Church zealous and enlightened ministers, and make their ministry more fruitful.

She tells them that from the moment they cease to direct their good works to these truly Apostolic ends, they no longer do what God expects from them, and cease to fulfil the purpose for which they were brought to Carmel.

The Carmelite nuns, daughters of St. Teresa, carry out in the cloister the ends proposed to them by their holy mother. They promote by their prayers and good works the spirit which St. Cajetan and so many holy ministers of the Church spread by their ministry. In addition to the many other religious orders they possess, who are engaged in active duties, such as the care of the sick, or the instruction of the children of the rich and poor, the people of Cork have the blessing of a new foundation of Carmelite nuns. Like the holy house of Nazareth, they, under the protection of the Blessed Virgin and St. Joseph, guard in their little chapel the infant Jesus. They spend their lives in returning thanks to God in the most Holy Sacrament. By their care this book is published, that devotion to St. Cajetan may be spread in this city. By their prayers, they promote the spirit he promoted.

Their chapel is open to the public, where from the noise of the world the faithful may come into the presence of Jesus exposed to their adoration in the most Holy Sacrament. The profits arising from the sale of this book will be devoted to helping them in their pious undertaking. They take this opportunity of thanking the Catholics of Cork for the uniform support, and the many acts of kindness received since their coming amongst them, and above all for the kind interest shown in their welfare by his Lordship, the Right Rev. Dr. Delany, who has gladly given his approbation to this book.

CARMELITE CONVENT, CORK,
Feast of the Patronage of St. Joseph,
May the 4th, 1873.

THE LIFE OF SAINT CAJETAN;

OR, GAËTAN OF THIENE.

———•———

IF the life of ordinary saints be full of instruction and edification, to those who deavour by such studies to advance in the career of Christian perfection, still more should we endeavour to collect every possible detail of the biography of those Pastors and Bishops of the Church who have become, by their zeal and holiness, founders of distinct religious orders, and thus added such lustre to their sacred profession. Among men like these, few have been more eminent than St. Gaëtan; although perhaps he is less known in England than St. Francis, St. Dominic, or St. Benedict, whose children are so widely spread over all lands that their dress and their rule have become familiar to us all. But, if the religion of a people depend on the holiness of

B

their priests, it is surely one of the greatest works to found and cement such orders of clergy as shall raise the tone and character of the priesthood, and this was one of the principal labours of St. Gaëtan, as it was of St. Charles Borromeo, and others.

He was born at Vincenza, in the Venetian territory, in the year 1480. His father was Gaspar, Count of Thiene, and his mother, Mary Porta, was also of one of the noblest families in Lombardy: but both were as remarkable for their piety as for their high rank. From the moment of his birth, the young Gaëtan was offered by his holy mother to the Blessed Virgin, to whom she had the greatest devotion; and our Lady accepted her offering and took the little child under her special protection, so that from his very infancy he seemed to be endowed with special grace, and was beyond his years both in goodness and knowledge. He had been named Gaëtan at his baptism out of respect to the memory of a great uncle, who bore that name, a canon of Padua, and one of the most famous theological professors of his day.

It is a trite observation that most great men owe their noblest qualities to the influence of their mothers.

The pious Countess of Thiene devoted herself to the education of our saint with all the zeal which her love for him inspired, and never ceased setting before his eyes the example of our Divine Redeemer's humility, meekness, purity, and other virtues. But her own daily life, and continual practice of self-denial and charity, worked more powerfully on the mind of her boy than all her exhortations. He saw that religion was to her a *reality;* the moving principle, in fact, of her whole life; and such was his docility to her teaching, that from his cradle he was called by his nurses the "little saint." When he was quite a child he lost his father, who commanded a body of cavalry, in a battle fought by the troops of Sixtus V., under General Malatesta, on the 22nd of August, 1482, in which he was grievously wounded; and died soon after, leaving the Countess of Thiene sole guardian of their children, the eldest of whom was but eight years old. When the first burst of natural grief was over, the poor widowed mother felt that she must now redouble her efforts on their behalf; and her whole life was henceforth spent in devotion to her fatherless little ones. But, with Gaëtan she had no difficulty. The principle of obedience seemed to be so rooted in his nature that it never occurred to him to dispute either her will, or that of the tutors whom she appointed over him. His compassion and love for the poor were such, that he denied himself every childish pleasure to be able to relieve them; and when he had exhausted all his own stores, he would beseech his mother with tears to give him the means of helping them more effectually. He had even to be watched so as to ensure his taking sufficient nourishment, as he had a thousand ingenious devices for concealing a portion of his dinner or supper, so as to give it to the poor children who flocked round the palace gates, as he went in and out.

The unalterable sweetness of his temper seemed to be the natural result of his constitution. As he grew older, the love of prayer and a spirit of constant recollection made him shun all loss of time, either in amusement or in idle conversation. Everything seemed to be uninteresting to him save his studies and church ceremonies, in which he took a marvellous pleasure. To serve mass, to deck the church with fresh flowers, or to take part in any of the imposing functions on holy-days or great festivals, was his greatest delight. His gentleness, modesty, and sweetness, endeared him to every one around him ; but especially to his mother, who would often praise and bless God for the way in which He had fulfilled her fondest hopes in this child.

But his life of prayer and constant recollection did not interfere with his progress in his studies; on the contrary, they only served to strengthen his powers and purify his judgment. That habit of concentration of mind on any particular subject resultad in his attaining to a wonderful degree of eminence in whatever he undertook. After a time, his mother sent him to complete his education at the University of Padua, where he soon outstripped all his companions ; while, by his irreproachable conduct, he won the esteem and respect of the Professors, who held him up as an example to the whole College. So far from being puffed up by their praise he became only more and more humble and devout. After having gone through the courses of philosophy and history, he devoted himself to the study of civil and canon law, in which faculty he took the degree of doctor, which was conferred upon him with unusual honour ou the 17th of July, 1504. After this, he gave himself up entirely to the study of divinity, and with his mother's full consent, determined to embrace the ecclesiastical state. But first he returned home for a short time—and, during this brief holiday, he persuaded his elder brother, John Baptist, Count of Thiene, to build a beautiful church at Rampazzo, near their country home, for the benefit of the peasants who lived at a considerable distance from the parish church. This church was dedicated to Saint Mary Magdelene, and Gaëtan endowed it out of his own private fortune, and appointed a holy chaplain who should say a daily mass for the inhabitants. " Thus," as an old biographer of the saint expresses it, " he who was so greatly to edify the Church hereafter began as a youth by raising a sanctuary to the honour and glory of Him to whom his whole life was henceforth to be devoted."

It is to be regretted that we have no further details of his early manhood; but his humility threw a veil over all his actions, and the secrets of this beautiful and hidden life were known but to his confessor and to God.

Having thus provided, as far as he could, for the spiritual welfare of the peasantry near his old home, he gave himself up altogether to the preparation for his reception of Holy Orders. During this time he was a model to all the other candidates, from his wonderful spirit of prayer, his devotion to the Blessed Sacrament, and his unwearied care of the sick and suffering. He resided in a parish of Vincenza itself, where, by the fervour of his exhortations and his extraordinary love of God, he, in spite of his youth, converted the whole town. Every one flocked to hear and see him, till his humility becoming alarmed, he resolved to retire privately from a place where he was so well known and where his family was so much esteemed, and go to Rome. He was strengthened in this purpose by his extreme anxiety to pray at the tombs of the Apostles; and also, by his wish to lead a hidden life, and advance more secretly in the way of perfection. But his extraordinary piety, together with his learning and high rank, soon brought him into notice, and the Pope, Julian II, discovering the eminent treasure whom God had placed within his reach, appointed him Prothonotary Apostolic, one of the highest dignities in the Roman Prelacy. This elevation did not suit Gaëtan's views or wishes in any way, but he was compelled to obey. Finding resistance impossible, his first care was to endeavour, by precept and example, to reform the manners and habits of the Papal Court by which he was surrounded, so as to conform them more nearly to the Christian maxims of mortification and holy poverty. There was at that time at Rome a congregation called of " The Divine Love," which was established in the Church of St. Sylvester and St. Dorothy, and the principal object of which was to kindle in men's hearts a more fervent love of God, and to check that luxury, libertinage, and love of pleasure, which were the characteristics of the age. Gaëtan at once enrolled himself in this holy congregation, which numbered among its members some of the most illustrious families in Rome. No sooner had he joined them than he infused into the whole body a wonderful new life, and a determination to work out not only their own perfection but that of their neighbours. Frequent communion was then almost unheard of, and the very best people never dreamt of approaching the Holy Table more than three or four times a year. But Gaëtan remonstrated with the members of the Congregation of " Divine Love " so strongly on this subject, that very soon monthly, then weekly, and even in some cases daily communions were the result; while their example greatly influenced others, and this holy practice began to spread into other places, to the great spiritual profit of the faithful.

The Pope, more and more delighted with Gaëtan's zeal and fervour, hastened his final consecration to the Divine service, and by a Brief *d'extra tempora* conferred upon him the four grades on four successive days, that is, on the 27th, 28th, 29th and 30th of September, he being then thirty-three years old. He had prepared himself for these solemn acts by an entire immolation of his body, soul, and spirit to the service of God ; and when once invested with the sacred offiice of priest, he prepared himself for the first celebration of the Holy Mysteries with so vivid a faith and love, and so profound a humility, that he amazed everyone around him. Jesus Christ seemed to have taken possession of his whole heart ; and by the entire mortification of his passions, and his wonderful purity of intention, he seemed (as his biographer states) "less a man than a seraph at the altar."

It was during this time that a singular and extra-ordinary grace was vouchsafed to him. Having gone on Christmas-eve to pray in the Church of Sta. Maria

Maggiore, Our Lord revealed Himself to him as a Baby, and the Blessed Virgin placed Him in Gaëtan's arms, "so that he might actually touch the corporal frame of the 'Word made flesh' and tangibly feel His presence."

He thus describes this wonderful favour in a letter to Sister Laura, a nun of the Convent of the Holy Cross at Brescia. And in this way he is often represented in his pictures. It is not difficult to guess how such a vision must have inflamed the Divine Love in his heart, and strengthened his resolve to devote his whole life to the "Little Babe of Bethlehem." It was about this time that he contracted a warm friendship with a gentleman named Barthelemi Stella, who was a member of the Congregation of "Divine Love." This gentleman, writing to a pious religious of his own family, says : "I have been advised to make the acquaintance of a wonderful servant of God here, the Count Gaëtan of Thiene, who left his family, came to Rome, and has become a priest, although now an only son, and the idol of his mother. He is thirty-four years old, wonderfully clever, very rich, and a devoted minister of the altar." This letter was addressed to *Laura Mignani*, a fervent Augustinian Nun, who afterwards died in the odour of sanctity; and it was through Barthelemi Stella that Gaëtan became acquainted with her. Although it does not appear that they ever met in life, they carried on a regular correspondence on spiritual subjects, which was an immense help and comfort to both. The follow·· ing is an extract from one of the letters which Gaëtan wrote to her at that time from Rome :—

" I have every day the inexpressible consolation of approaching Him who has said : ' Learn of me for I am meek and lowly of heart; ' and yet I am still full of pride. I receive every day Him who came 'to bring fire and a sword,' and yet I am cold and idle, and still cling to earthly affections. I have the boldness to offer Him, from whom the sun itself receives its light, and who has created the whole world ! What wonderful love to be chosen a minister to such a God ! Oh ! pray for me that my icy soul may become a fiery furnace."

. . . . . He then describes the vision we have mentioned above, and continues : " I believe my heart must be as hard as a diamond not to have melted at such a moment ! "

St. Gaëtan's estimate of himself proves what was the

humility of one who was already looked upon as the glory of the priesthood and the reviver of the sanctuary.

Ten years had elapsed since Gaëtan had arrived in Rome, when, on the death of Pope Julian, he found himself at liberty to return to Vicenxa, where the failing health of his mother, and the death of his elder brother, rendered his presence in every way desirable. He writes to Laura " that his return seemed to have given new life to his holy and venerable parent." But he was soon called upon by God to sacrifice this the fondest affection of his heart on earth. The Countess received for only a short time at the sight of her favourite child, and very soon all the bad symptoms returned. Gaëtan thus describes her last illness in a letter to Lanra :—

" During all her sufferings, which were at times excessive, no trace of sadness appeared on her countenance. She, who had edified us all during her whole life, was to give us proofs of equal piety up to her latst breath. She never omitted any of her usual acts of devotion, and even practised several mortifications. During the whole of her last illness, which lasted fifteen days, the Holy Sacrifice of the Mass was offered up every day at the foot of her bed, in which she assisted with the utmost fervour. She had the happiness of receiving the Holy Communion four or five times, and would have done so every day if she had been able."

After describing her edifying end, and touching on his own sorrow, he adds: "that his only fear is lest she should have sinned through too sensible an affection for himself, and from not having sufficiently warned him of his faults." He recommends her earnestly to the prayers of the nuns at Brescia; but, it appears from one of the old Chronicles, that while he was weeping and praying by her inanimate remains that night, he received by revelation the happy assurance that she had escaped passing through Purgatory through his intercession. Scarcely were these last and touching duties accomplished than, with renewed zeal, he devoted himself to his sacerdotal duties; and, among other things, enrolled himself in a congregation which he found established in Vincenza, that of St. Jerome. His family endeavoured to dissuade him from taking this step, as the congregation was composed almost entirely of artisans and poor. But as he sought for neither grandeur nor the esteem of men, but only a means of advancing in virtue, he laughed at their remonstrances, and inscribed

his name among these poor people with the greater
pleasure that it drew down upon him the scorn of those
of his own class. It is impossible to over estimate the
good that he did in this congregation. He continually
invited them to conferences and little exhortations, in
which he spoke with such unction and such wonderful
love of God, that his audience would often melt into
tears, and nothing could resist his influence over them. ·
On the subject of the Blessed Eucharist, especially, he
seemed to have an inexhaustible eloquence. And his
words had such an effect on these poor people that they
adopted the custom of receiving the Holy Communion
three and four times a week; and in all ways began to
lead new and devout lives, in accordance with his
teaching and example. Not content, however, with the
effect he had produced on their minds, he desired to
associate them also in active works of charity; and for
that purpose persuaded them to undertake the care of
the Incurable Hospital, which was affiliated to that of
St. James at Rome, and considered one of the best in
Italy. Gaëtan added greatly to the size and comfort of
the building, and went from house to house, to seek out
the sick and miserable, and convey them to the new

Hospital, where he tended them himself with the greatest devotion. No disease however loathsome, and no service however revolting to the senses, ever seemed to deter him in these pious offices. He made their beds himself, dressed their wounds, washed their linen, &c., but above all, never missed the opportunity of reconciling them to God, and preparing them for a holy and edifying death. The Rector of the congregation of St. Jerome, John Dominic Zaninelli, having ventured to represent to him that he was exhausting his resources altogether by the munificence of his alms, he made this heroic answer: " I shall never cease to give all I can to the poor and suffering, until the time comes when I shall be so despoiled of my goods that I shall have to be buried by charity."

About this time, Gaëtan, whose humility made him always doubt his own judgment, put himself under the direction of a holy Dominican Father, Jean Baptiste de Crème. By his advice, Gaëtan went to Verona, where the Members of the Oratory of St. Syr wished to be united to the congregation of St. Jerome, and participate in their good works. He begged to be enrolled among the St. Syr Oratorians, and inscribed his name in that confraternity on the 10th July, 1519, as " *Gaëtan, unworthy priest.*" His advice and exhortations had as much weight at Verona as in his native town : but he devoted himself especially to the poor, encouraging them to bear all their trials with faith and patience.

On his return to Vincenza, he gave up living in his own palace, and took up his abode in the Incurable Hospital, so as to be able to devote himself more entirely to his " dear patients, " as he termed them. He did not, however, neglect the duties of his position as head of a noble family ; for we find him soon after engaged in the establishment of his brother's only child, the Countess Elizabeth of Thiene, who married Count Porto, on the 22nd of April, 1521, at which marriage Gaëtan performed the ceremony. He wrote to her, soon after, a beautiful letter of advice on the duties of her new position, and the urgent need of her sanctifying herself in the world by the frequentation of the sacraments. " How much those art to be pitied," he continued, " who do not realise the blessing of the Holy Eucharist ! We may possess our Lord Jesus Christ, and we will not ! Woe to that soul who can be thus indifferent to receive her God and Saviour ! The

enemies of our salvation suggests doubts and difficulties
only that they may obtain a triumph over us. Let us
hasten to receive Him, who, in giving Himself to us, is
ready also to give us all the graces of which we stand in
need."

But even in the holiest lives there are moments of
darkness and perplexity, and Gaëtan was not to be
exempt from such trials. He writes to his venerable
friend, Laura, on the 8th of June, 1520 : " I am much
troubled as to the future, and cannot make up my mind
whether I shall give up my charge (of Protonotary
Apostolic) and remain in my own country ; or leave it.
I feel as if my path at present were all darkness. . . .
But I have only one wish and that is to do the will of
God in whatever place or way He may appoint. I feel
that He demands of me a complete sacrifice of myself,
and I am willing to obey. It is not only by fervour of
feeling but by fervour in action that we attain to entire
detachment of purity and heart."

His obedience was soon to be put to the test in a way
which he little expected. In the very midst of his great
work at the Hospital, where his presence seemed abso-
lutely necessary to the very existence of the charity, his

Director suddenly told him to give up everything and go
and live at Venice. Gaëtan obeyed with the simplicity
of a child, and, disregarding all human considerations
and the remonstrances of every one around him, left Vincenza and his home, and after the manner of Abraham,
" went into a strange country." He confesses that in so
doing he acted entirely contrary to his own judgment,
as he feared that his new congregation would greatly
suffer by his absence. But, if Vincenza sorrowed for the
saint's departure, Venice was no less rejoiced at his
arrival. He made no change in his habits or way of
life, lodging at the new hospital, which had just been
built, and introducing into it by degrees all the improve-
ments he had carried out at Vincenza. Before many
weeks had elapsed he became the friend, the consoler,
and the adviser of every one in Venice who was in need
of aid. But what astonished the people more than anything else was to see a man of his high rank and position, after labouring day and night among the sick and
suffering, live upon little else than bread and water, and
wear a ragged cassock and an old cloak which the poorest
village curate would have disdained. The Venetians
profited much by this example of self-abnegation, and

attributed to his prayers their escape from the terrible disasters inflicted by the Turks at that time on the neighbouring provinces. He himself, however, was not so well satisfied with the Venetians. He wrote to Paul Justiniani, the reformer of the Camaldoli Monastery, in the following terms: " Although this city is a beautiful one, and full of every kind of attraction, one can only weep over her : for the people are dead to sentiments of piety ; no one dares publicly come to confession or communion. I shall never be happy till I see Christians hungering for this Divine Food ! " But his Director, although marvelling more and more at the spiritual progress of his beloved disciple, and at the good everywhere effected by his presence, felt convinced that Venice was not a proper sphere for his labours, and that he was destined by God to do great works, not only for individual towns, but for the universal Church. He, therefore, a second time, desired him to break up his home and go to Rome.

Gaëtan obeyed with the same ready alacrity ; and returning to his old congregation of " Divine Love," resolved to devote himself with greater zeal than ever to the reform of the clergy. The civil wars which had

ravaged all Christendom had more or less demoralised
every class in society, and the abuses which had crept
in among the clergy were so great that it might have
been said in the words of the Prophet: " A planta pedis
usque ad verticem, non est in ea sanitas." Gaëtan,
therefore, conceived the project of forming a congregation of Evangelical Priests, whose one and only aim
would be to save souls. A great friend of his, Boniface
de Colle, warmly seconded him in this pious enterprise.
Peter Caraffa, Bishop of Théate, in the kingdom of
Naples, and Archbishop of Brindisi, heard of Gaëtan's
design, and entreated to be allowed to give up his ecclesiastical dignities and join him. St. Gaëtan at first
refused, representing to him the importance of the
charges he then held, and the great loss which would
accrue to his flock from the absence of such a pastor.
But Caraffa (who had acted as Papal Nuncio in England and Spain, and as Regent of the latter country
under Charles V,) was more and more determined to
put himself under St. Gaëtan's guidance, and so impor-
tuned the Pope, Clement VII, to allow him to resign
his high functions. The Pope naturally objected to his
proposal ; but, finally, was won over by the disinterested

entreaties of one whose only object was to extend the
kingdom of God in the hearts of men. Paul Consigliéri,
a great friend of Caraffa's, of the noble Roman family of
Gislheri, and a member of the Roman Senate, determined to follow his example; and so these four noblemen, " being united in one heart and one soul " (as their
old biographer states) determined to relinquish all their
dignities, and, binding themselves by solemn vows, to
form a congregation which should be entitled simply of
" *Regular Clergy.*"

The first thing to be done was to obtain the Papal
approbation of their new Order. This was attended with
some difficulties. The Roman Prelates looked upon the
whole movement as a singular innovation, and, especially objected to the clause which prohibited their receiving ecclesiastical revenues. St. Gaëtan, however, stuck
to his point. He asserted that the only wish of himself
and his associates was to imitate the lives of the Apostles, who had no certain revenues, and that priests bound
by solemn vows would edify the Church all the more as
they were detached from all worldly ties or riches.
Matthew Ghiberti, Bishop of Verona, finally induced the
Pope to listen to their petition and grant the Bull of

approbation. This being obtained, they separated for three or four months in order to arrange their worldly affairs. But on the 14th of September, 1524, the day of the exaltation of the Holy Cross, these four holy founders, having renounced their dignities and all their worldly goods (of which the poor had the largest share), made their solemn profession in the Church of St. Peter, on the Vatican Hill; Bonziero, Bishop of Caserta, having been deputed by the Pope to receive their vows. They proceeded at once to the election of a Superior, which fell upon Caraffa, whom the Pope insisted should keep his dignity of Bishop of Théate. Hence the name given to these religious of " *Théatins.*"

The principal objects of their institution were as follows :

1. To set an example to the clergy, who at that time were often living bad and disorderly lives.

2. To give an example of perfect poverty.

3. To restore the beauty and cleanliness of the altars and churches, and the pomp of the Divine ceremonies, which, from neglect and want of reverence, had become a perfect scandal to the heretics.

4. To kindle in the hearts of the faithful a keener

desire for the frequentation of the Sacraments, which had fallen into such disuse that the greater portion of the people went to confession only once a year, and that without contrition or purpose of amendment of life.

5. To preach the Word of God, which at that time was often mingled in the pulpit with profane and even ridiculous subjects.

6. To visit the sick and prepare the dying for the last Sacraments.

7. To accompany criminals to the place of execution, so as to save their souls, if possible, from eternal chastisements.

8. To counteract and combat the heresies which had sprung up in Germany and elsewhere through the apostacy of Luther and his disciples.

After this solemn profession, the four friends retired to a house belonging to Boniface de Collo, a little outside Rome, on what was called Il Campo di Marzo. Here they joined the exercises of a contemplative with an active life, and edified the whole city of Rome by their indefatigable charity; so much so, that when the people wished to describe any one of eminent piety they would say, " *He is as holy as a Théatin.*" A number of novices joined them towards the end of the year, so that they were compelled to remove to a larger house on the Monte Pincio. The love of God and the wish to make Him known and loved by all men, was the bond of union which made this little band of workers irresistible.

But this new order was destined to be strangely tried by an event which at that time carried ruin and desolation throughout Italy. On the 6th of May, 1527, Rome was besieged by Charles, Connétable de Bourbon, who had betrayed the service of his master, Francis the First, and gone over to that of Charles the Fifth. The army was composed of every kind of barbarian and heretic, and they, exasperated by the death of the Constable, (mortally wounded during the siege) committed every sort of excess, horror, and sacrilege in the capital of Christendom. The Théatins multiplied themselves to succour the wounded, to aid the dying, to bury the dead, and to console the inhabitants, whom the cruelty and rapacity of the conquerors had rendered almost desperate. Gaëtan alone performed prodigies of charity during this terrible time. But being unhappily recognized by one of the soldiers, who had known him at

Vincenza, and imagined the apparent poverty of their house to be only feigned, he was put to the torture in order to force him to reveal the gold he was supposed to have concealed; hung up by his feet, his fingers squeezed between the lids of a chest, and his whole body torn with whips. His companions were treated with similar barbarity, and at last thrown into a loath-some dungeon. Their patience and courage under these terrible sufferings amazed their inhuman persecutors; and when, after the example of the Apostles, they com-menced singing the praises of God in their prison, this act brought about their deliverance, for, the officer in command, overhearing them, desired to be admitted into their dungeon, and was so struck with the dignity and modesty of their behaviour, that he ordered their instant release.

The terrible state of Rome at that moment induced them for a time to leave the city and strive elsewhere to exercise their ministry. They embarked on board a fisherman's boat on the Tiber for Ostia, but were fired on by an officer who thought they were carrying off some treasure, till he fortunately recognised one of the party as his nephew, and instantly overwhelmed them

with kindnesses, and provided them with the provisions
necessary for their voyage. At Ostia they found another
protector in Dominic Veniero, Venetian Ambassador at
Rome; and in the Commander of the Venetian Fleet,
Augustine Amuléo, who gave them a free passage on
board his vessel, which carried them safely to Venice.
There they were received with open arms by the
Republic and lodged, first at St. Euphemia, then at St.
George's on the Great Canal, and, finally, at St. Nicolas
de Tolentino, where a house and church were assigned
to them, of which they took possession on the 29th of
September, 1527, and where their Order has remained
to this day.

During their stay at St. George's, the three years
superiorship of the Bishop of Théate having expired, St.
Gaëtan was unanimously chosen in his place. The
wonders that he did at Venice for the reform of both
clergy and people are dwelt upon at great length by his
biographers, and a new occasion for showing his pastoral
zeal soon presented itself in a fearful plague, which
ravaged the city and spread such terror among all
classes that none but the Théatins could be found to
administer to the dying and the dead. A famine fol-

lowed this terrible visitation of God, and Gaëtan seemed
to forget that he was the father of his religious to become the father of the starving multitude around him.
Poor as he was himself, he found means to relieve thou-
sands who would otherwise have died of hunger; and by
his exhortations and entreaties opened the purses of the
rich, and induced them to contribute liberally to their
wants. Scarcely was this great distress over, than he
was summoned to Verona to settle a quarrel which had
arisen between the Bishop of that town and his flock,
and succeeded in arranging matters to the satisfaction of
both parties. On his return to Venice, the Bishop of
Théate being again elected Superior, Gaëtan went back
with fresh pleasure to the care of the sick in the Incurable
Hospital; and, also, devoted himself to inspiring a
stronger love for the Blessed Sacrament in the minds of
the people. For this purpose he instituted the "Forty
Hours" Adoration; and also a Grand Novena at
Christmas to honour the Incarnation of Our Blessed
Lord. He decreed likewise that, at sunset, after the
"Angelus," a pause should be made to pray for the dead,
which custom is followed in many towns of Italy to this
day. He was also empowered by the Pope to correct

certain abuses which had crept into the Breviary and
Missal, in which several changes were proposed by St.
Gaëtan, which were approved of by Clement VII in a special Brief. He was most careful in the selection of those
who were to join his Congregation ; and, on one occasion, when a gentleman of high birth and great talent
offered himself as a novice on certain conditions, Gaëtan
refused him in an admirable letter, in which he pointed
out the necessity of all who entered his Institute being
ready to submit their wills unreservedly to the Superior,
as the representative to them of Jesus Christ, and con-
cluded with the words: " Humility is a better passport
for admission among us than temporal goods or great
talents. We do not despise learning ; but we care more
that those who embrace our rule should be animated
with the spirit of God. ' Knowledge puffeth up, but
charity edifieth.' "

A short time after, our saint was chosen by the Pope
to open a House of their Order at Naples. The Bishop
of Théate begged him to select whichever of his companions he preferred to accompany him. The humility
of St. Gaëtan took alarm at this proposal : " What," he
exclaimed, " I am to choose the person I like best ?

No, no; it is not thus one practises holy obedience ; on the contrary, I will pray to our Lord (turning to a Crucifix on the table) that He may inspire your reverence with the thought to send the father who shall be the least congenial to my taste and humour."

The Bishop's admiration of St. Gaëtan was only increased by these words, and he assigned to him as companion his favourite disciple, Jean Marinon, who was not only a devout priest but an excellent preacher. They started for Rome in the dog-days, and went to kiss the Pope's feet on their way and to crave his blessing. The Pope, seeing them almost scorched by the heat of the sun, exclaimed : "How is it, my children, that you have set out at this season at the risk of your lives? "

St. Gaëtan replied : "Holy Father, it were better for us to die on the road than to hesitate a single day in obeying your commands."

The Pope was greatly touched at their zeal, and gave them the most flattering reception. The pious Bishop of Verona joyfully received them in his own palace at Rome. But they only stayed a few days, being anxious to begin their new mission and not disappoint the Count

d'Oppido, who had prepared everything at Naples for
their reception. Finding, however, that the house
chosen by the Count was too far from the town, they
resolved to seek another lodging ; but met with great
opposition from their determination not to accept lands
or revenues. The Count represented to St. Gaëtan how
impossible it would be for so large a community to continue to exist without definite means—that the present
charity of the people would cool—and that then they
would be left destitute. Failing in moving the Saint's
determination, the Count sent some noted religious of
other Orders to convince him. Gaëtan asked them :
" How they could be certain of being maintained ? "
They replied : " That they had lands and houses secured
to them by lease." " Well," answered the Saint, " we
have a better contract than you, for we have the pro-
mise of Jesus Christ, ' Seek ye first the kingdom of God
and His righteousness and all these things will be added
unto you.' Our Congregation has subsisted very well
at Venice for ten years in spite of the fearful famine
which has decimated Italy, and the same Providence
will sustain us at Naples." On the still further objec-
tion being made that " Naples was not so rich as

Venice," he replied : "*I believe that the God of Venice is equally the God of Naples.*"

To cut short their arguments, St. Gaëtan at last summoned his companions, and closing the doors of the house, and sending the keys to the Count, told them to take only their Breviaries with them and come into the town. Here they were received by a holy woman named Maria Lorenzo Longuo, a widow lady, and the Superior of the Hospital for Incurables, who offered them a little lodging in the Hospital, and welcomed them " as if they had been angels from on High," as Caraffa writes in a letter of thanks addressed to her from Venice. Soon after, she purchased an adjoining house for them, in which they built a chapel, which St. Gaëtan called " Sta. Maria della Stalla," from his great devotion to the mystery of the Crib of Bethlehem. St. Gaëtan became the Director of this holy Superior, and by his advice she gave up an intended journey to the Holy Land, and embraced the rule of St. Clare. She became afterwards the foundress of the Capucines in Naples, who, by their fervent and penitent lives, gave great edification to the Church. There was another lady, the Duchess d'Ayerbo de Tremoli, who listened eagerly to St. Gaëtan's teaching,

and who, in consequence of his advice, opened a
House of Refuge for penitent women ; one of the very
first of the kind which had been attempted. A third
Religious House (that of the "Sapienza") was also
inspired by St. Gaëtan, of which Maria Caraffa became
Superior, and thus revived the primitive spirit of St.
Dominic.

It would be tedious to our readers to detail all the
good which St. Gaëtan and his companions effected in
Naples, and especially among the priests, who began to
be ashamed of their irregular lives, and to imitate the
holy example of the Théatins. Several miracles worked
at this time by St. Gaëtan increased the veneration in
which he was already held by the people. A lay
brother having been seriously injured in a work he had
undertaken from obedience, was condemned by the surgeons to lose his leg. St. Gaëtan begged them to defer
the operation till the next day, and that night, going in to
the sufferer, he wiped the wound, made over it the sign
of the cross, and telling the sick brother to trust in God
and ask the aid of St. Francis, he returned to his cell,
and spent the rest of the night in prayer. The following morning when the surgeons came they found the

leg entirely healed and no sign of the fearful wounds of the day before.

Another of his Community, who had gone out of his mind, was also restored by St. Gaëtan's intercession. But he endeavoured to keep all those things as quiet as possible, and it was not until his canonization that these miracles were proved incontestably by the evidence of the doctors.

The Pope Paul III, who had succeeded Clement VII, having conferred a Cardinal's Hat on the Bishop of Théate, Gaëtan was obliged to go to Rome for a General Chapter of his Order. He appointed one of the most eminent of his Congregation as Superior in his place at Naples, Peter Foscarini. The humility of this true follower of St. Gaëtan shrank from the position, and he declared he had not sufficient authority to be Superior. St. Gaëtan replied: "My Father, you will have plenty of grace for the charge assigned to you if you strive to win the love in the Lord of those under you."

Finding that the house near the Incurable Hospital had become too small for them, the Vice-Roy assigned to the Théatins the Parish Church of St. Paolo Maggiore, with a house alongside, of which they took possession in 1538.

All the zeal, learning, and eloquence of St. Gaëtan were now called into play to answer and detect the heresies of three noted apostates, John Valdasio, Peter Vermiglio, and Bernardin Ochino, who, at that time, were filling Naples with their false doctrines. The first was a Lutheran, the second an Augustinian, and the third a Capuchin, whose vanity and ambition had induced them to rebel against the authority of the Church, and promulgate everywhere their heretical tenets. Gaëtan wrote to his Théatin Cardinal, and the apostates were summoned to Rome, but made their escape to Zurich, and soon after perished miserably.

The remaining years of St. Gaëtan's life were spent as Superior alternately at Venice, Verona, and Naples. But these changes did not in any way affect his way of life. It was always the same—severe to himself, but full of gentleness and sweetness towards others. His mortification of spirit was so great that when the Emperor Charles V passed through Naples on his return from Turin, and the magnificence of his reception exceeded anything that had ever been heard or thought of,

St. Gaëtan, who had only to open his window to see the whole procession, refrained, from the love of God, and spent the whole time in prayer. Never was there any man more possessed with the love of souls, or with a more ardent desire for the glory of God; so much so that he received the honourable name of " *Venator animarum.*" His spirit of prayer was such, that he would sometimes remain five or six hours on his knees, so absorbed in God that he forgot the time. Often he was favoured with wonderful visions and revelations during these ecstasies. On one occasion our Lord appeared to him covered with wounds; on another, bearing His Cross and inviting him to help Him. His principal devotions after those to our Lord were to his Blessed Mother; and he rarely mentioned the name of Jesus without adding " Son of Mary." He was also very devout to St. Andrew, on account of his ardent desire to suffer for Christ; and to St. Francis of Assisi, from his great love of holy poverty. The latter virtue he esteemed so highly that he nearly gave up his house at Verona because the bishop there would insist on overwhelming them with food and comforts. His own penances were continual. His temperance was so great that it may have been called a perpetual fast. He constantly wore a hair shirt, and took the discipline with such vehemence that it seemed as if his flesh were positively hateful to him; and he was once heard to say, "that he loathed it as he did the devil." Of his charity we have already spoken—his whole life was, in fact, an act of devotion to the poor and sick and suffering members of Christ's body. To sum up all in one word, he was one of those whose whole soul was absorbed in God, and who was entirely detached from all things here below; so much so, that, on one occasion, during his prayers, he confessed to feeling as if his heart had left his body and flown upwards to heaven.

During one of his visits to his old friend, Cardinal Caraffa, at Rome, he became acquainted with St. Ignatius Loyola, who was so touched by the fervour and zeal of the members of his institute that he wished to join them. But God had other designs for his servant, although the friendship those two saints contracted for each other from that moment never ceased. But if the zeal of good men was thus kindled in the Church during that century, the enemy of all good was busier than ever in stirring up heresies and rebellion against all spiritual authority.

A terrible sedition broke out in Naples in consequence of an attempt on the part of the Vice-Roy, Don Piétro di Toledo, to establish the Inquisition in that city. The people rose as one man against this tribunal, and the idea was abandoned ; but the rescue of a debtor by some young noblemen having fanned the flame, a civil war was the result. St. Gaëtan endeavoured to appease the tumult, though for a long time in vain. He caused public prayers to be said, and processions, singing lita-nies, to traverse the principal streets, with the addition of the following petition and antiphon :—

"Ut civitatem istam defendere, pacificare, custodire et conservare digneris, te rogamus, audi nos ! "

"Exaudi Domine, placare Domine, attende et fac, ne moreris propter temetipsum Deus meus, quia nomen tuum invocatum est super civitatum istam et super populum tuum."

After a time peace was restored ; but the evils of the Church did not thereby diminish. The Council of Trent, which had been convoked to condemn the new heresies and reform the errors in the Catholic body, was obliged to be dispersed for a time owing to the plague ; and there seemed no immediate prospect of any cessation of

the disorders which at that time afflicted all Christendom.

These great calamities so deeply affected St. Gaëtan
that he became dangerously ill; his health had likewise
been undermined by his extraordinary labours and aus-
terities, so that the doctor who was called in became
much alarmed, and desired to have a further opinion;
but St. Gaëtan refused. "As a poor religious I am too
thankful to have one doctor without calling in a second.
It is only too much to have the benefit of your skill."
The doctor then entreated him to allow himself to be
laid on a softer mattress. "*I* lie on a soft bed!" exclaimed the saint, "God forbid! When my Lord and
Saviour died on a Cross, I will only die on ashes."

He received the last sacraments with that fervour of
devotion which characterised all his actions. His spiritual children gathered eagerly round him, fearing to lose
any of his last words. Filled with the most profound
humility the saint turned to them and said: "I do not
know, my dear brethren, that I have ever offended any
one of you intentionally; at least, I do not remember
having done so; but if I have ever given pain to any one
I now most humbly beg his pardon." They all burst

into tears at these words, assuring him that he had always been to them as the tenderest father. He continued: "If I have lived as a poor man, and if I am now dying, by my own wish, in extreme poverty, it is because I have always so highly esteemed that virtue. I earnestly commend the love and practice of holy poverty to you all." He then exhorted them to pray for the grace of perseverance; to have no object save the glory of God and the salvation of souls; to combat energetically the heresies of the day; and, above all, to live in peace and unity among themselves. Then looking at his Crucifix with an expression of intense love, and with his eyes bathed in tears, he repeated the words of Daniel: "Placare, Domine, attende et fac!" and then breathed his last, without a struggle, on the 7th of August, 1547, in the twenty-third year of the foundation of his Order, and the sixty-seventh of his age.

His body was solemnly interred in the Church of St. Paul at Naples, where it is still held in the greatest veneration. On the day of his death the troubles of the town were suddenly appeased, which every one attributed to the effect of his powerful intercession with God; while an innumerable number of miracles attested his extraordinary sanctity.

An eye-witness of his daily life, Erasmus Danesi, a secular priest, has left us the following account of St. Gaëtan, which contains some details not already mentioned in these pages :—"I know not (he writes) how to describe one whose whole life was so exemplary. He was wonderfully humble, gentle, and modest, speaking little and praying much. Nothing could be more persuasive or more touching than his exhortations. It was impossible to prevent his doing the most menial work in the community. He was the first to rise at the sound of the bell for matins, and would remain prostrate before the Blessed Sacrament from the time office was over till he said his mass. His delicacy of conscience was such that he went to confession every day before going up to the altar. His frugality was excessive, and very often he dined on bread and fruit alone. He was most grateful to the benefactors of his missions, and would have their names written down and read out aloud to the Community that they might not be forgotten in their prayers. He had a peculiar tenderness towards any who were sick among his religious, nursed and attended to them himself, and would beg for anything for them which he could not procure. The furniture of his own cell was as poor as possible : a table, a chair, a Drie-pieu, a few old books, and a paper picture, were its only ornaments. He slept upon straw. His clothes were of the commonest and coarsest description. He was about the average height, and wore his hair very short according to the custom of the time. From the severity of his penances, and his perpetual abstinence, he was extremely thin; but his natural fresh colour remained. His face was round: his eyes large and full: and the greatest sweetness was expressed in his look and in his mouth, which attracted people at first sight."

Another of his biographers writes:

"Gaëtan, who appeared to us all as an angel of God when praying or officiating at the altar, and whose touching eloquence no one could resist, was in his own sight 'a very worm and the outcast of the people.' He always reminded me of those words of our Lord: 'My meat is to do the will of Him that sent me,' for it was really true that the winning of souls was to him as meat and drink, and at such times he would forget all else. Half his nights were spent in prayer. Poor and humble as he was in his own person and cell, he was never satisfied with anything less than splendour in the decoration of his churches, and in all that pertained to the Divine

Worship. That arose partly from his intense devotion
to the Blessed Sacrament, for the honouring of which
nothing was too costly or too beautiful. In his quality
of Superior, he enforced authority and obedience solely
by love and by his own example. He had a wonderful
discrimination of character, and such good judgment
that his advice was eagerly sought for on all sides.
Nothing seemed to ruffle his peace and inward tran-
quillity. In any emergency he would use his utmost
endeavours to bring about the desired result; but,
having done that, he would leave the issue to God without any further trouble or anxiety. So great was his
humility that he refused to receive the visits of his rich
and noble relations, saying, 'that they came with too
much pomp.' Everything about him showed an angeli-
cal purity, and he rarely lifted his eyes from the ground
in the presence of women. If any wonderful cures were
the result of his prayers, he would always strive to
attribute them to other causes, or to the intercession of
some saint. In a word, his life was hid with Christ in
God, and with Him he is gone to reign for ever and for
ever."

The many miracles worked on his tomb brought about

his beatification by Pope Urban VIII, and his canonization afterwards by Pope Clement X, on the 12th of
April, 1671. He is specially venerated at Naples, of
which town he is one of the principal patrons. His
houses were quickly multiplied in Italy, Sicily, Spain,
and Germany, and although no branch of the Théatins
exists in Paris, yet great devotion is felt for St. Gaëtan
among the Capuchins at Marseilles, the Augustinians at
Amiens, and the Carmelites at St. Denys. The latter
placed their infirmary under his patronage, and had the
principal events of his life represented on their walls.
May we not consider St. Gaëtan the special protector
of these spouses of Jesus Christ, among whom the
Princess Louise of France was one of the most fervent
and saintly ?

St. Gaëtan was at first buried, by his own desire, in
the common cemetery of the Théatins, and without any
peculiar distinction ; but a few years after his death,
his body was removed to the crypt of St. Paul, where
a chapel was afterwards built and dedicated to him. A
handsome staircase leads down into this chapel where
his remains rest, together with those of his faithful disciple the Blessed Marinon. His letters have been carefully

preserved in the different houses of the Théatins, and the same spirit of disinterestedness and zeal for the glory of God still marks the Order of which he was the founder.

We cannot do better than conclude our biography of this eminent servant of God in the words of the Rev. P. de Gracy, one of his own congregation, from whose life of the saint the principal facts related in this history are taken.

"St. Gaëtan lived only for God and for the salvation of his neighbour. Do you, my reader, look upon life in the same way?

"St. Gaëtan was the father of the poor and served them with his own hands. Do you visit the sick and the suffering yourself, and endeavour, as far as you can, to relieve them?

"St. Gaëtan was specially devoted to the Blessed Sacrament, and full of fervour in the daily celebration of the Holy Sacrifice.

"How often do you assist at mass, and with what dispositions?

"St. Gaëtan, notwithstanding the innocence and purity of his life, practised the severest mortifications.

What penance do you inflict upon yourself for your faults? and how do you watch over your senses?

To die like the just, you must live as they did. And thus alone can you hope to reign with them for ever in the kingdom of our Lord."

MAXIMS;

OR,

SENTENCES OF ST. GAËTAN:

Taken from his Biography, by the Rev. P. D. G. Silos.

———————

1. Pious exercises are a necessary means to maintain a religious spirit in the heart, but the essence of religion consists in an entire conformity of our will to the will of God.

2. All the enjoyments of this life are deceptive, because they do not satisfy, but only puff one up; God alone who made our hearts can fill them with consolations.

3. He who fully realises his own vileness in the sight of God, will naturally be patient, gentle, and sweet, in dealing with his neighbour.

4. No one should be foolish enough to meddle in

affairs which do not concern him. It is a sufficiently grave responsibility to have to render an account to God of all our special obligations.

5. A Christian who lives in forgetfulness of his true country, which is Heaven, is like a traveller who, blinded by drink, cannot find his way home.

6. He who has the most care for his own life and most esteem for himself, feels most the weight of human misery.

7. If we study with all our hearts to please God, we shall find Him ever ready to remember us in all our necessities.

8. Never let us forget that as, day by day, we draw nearer to the end of our mortal life, we ought to rejoice, because we are drawing so much nearer to the beginning of eternity.

9. Never let us trust in our own merits, or in the certainty of our eternal salvation, for God alone holds in His hand the grace of final perseverance.

10. To be satisfied with not being in mortal sin is the worst peril for a soul, because the most insidious; and is a real offence against the infinite love and mercy of God.

11. Let us fear lest by deceiving ourselves in over-indulging our bodies, we become really cruel towards our souls.

12. In combating our infernal enemy let us always consider ourselves as new and untried soldiers, without arms and full of worldly affections; above all, let us remember that he never sleeps.

NOVENA FOR THE FEAST OF ST. GAETAN.

———•———

In the name of the Father, Son, and Holy Ghost. Amen.

1. Glorious saint, who at the sacred crib wast favoured with an angelic vision, and with the presence of the Holy Child and of His blessed mother, deign to guard, console, and protect my soul.

Pater, Ave, Gloria.

2. Glorious saint, who by thy merits wast permitted to see the bread changed into flowers which thou hadst hidden for the poor, beseech our Lord to fill my heart with a true charity towards my neighbour.

Pater, Ave, Gloria.

3. Glorious saint, who didst receive from the Holy Spirit the gift of peace in the visible form of a dove, beseech our Lord to grant me strength to resist my evil

passions, and resign myself in all my labours and troubles to the Divine will.

Pater, Ave, Gloria.

4. Glorious saint, who didst receive in thine arms from the Blessed Virgin, the Holy Child Jesus, pray for me that I may have but a spark of that love with which thine own soul was filled for our most amiable Redeemer.

Pater, Ave, Gloria.

5. Glorious saint, who relying entirely on Divine Providence, wert frequently relieved in thy dire necessities by the special ministrations of angels, pray that I may have a firm and unwavering trust in God's mercy.

Pater, Ave, Gloria.

6. Glorious saint, who, absorbed in Divine contemplation, felt thy whole heart enclosed in that of the Redeemer, obtain for me an ardent wish to be continually united to Him, and to detach myself more and more from the things of this world.

Pater, Ave, Gloria.

7. Glorious saint, who, wrapped in ecstacy, wert admitted to taste of the joy of the pure heart of Mary,

and to partake of the ineffable sweetness of her Son Jesus, obtain for me a thorough purity of heart and intention.

Pater, Ave, Gloria.

8. Glorious saint, who wast permitted in spirit to feel some of the bitter pains of our Lord on the cross, pray that I may be inspired with the same thirst as thyself to suffer with Jesus Christ and to be crucified with Him.

Pater, Ave, Gloria.

Glorious saint, whose death was mainly caused by thy sorrow for the sins of others, and who at thy last passage wast cheered by the presence of Mary, who called thee to a glorious throne in the kingdom of her Son, obtain for me a hearty sorrow for my many sins and shortcomings, and that grace which I most need, so that I may arrive at eternal life.

Pater, Ave, Gloria.

Ora pro nobis, Beatæ Cajetane.

Ut digni efficiamur, etc.

Oremus.

Omnipotens sempiterne Deus, qui S. Cajetanum Confessorum mirabiliter in tua Providentia confidentem, terrena fecisti despicere, et donis cœlestibus abundare, concede propitius, ut qui ejus commemorationem colimus, cœlestis ejusdem Providentiæ præsidia sentiamus, et ad sempiterna jugiter aspiremus. Per Christum, &c.

Note.—This Novena was published at Vincenza on the 5th of August, 1871, on the occasion of the second centenary of his canonization.

www.ingramcontent.com/pod-product-compliance
Lightning Source LLC
Chambersburg PA
CBHW022157020726
47496CB00008B/2758